Adventures in Steam Books

Published by Adventures in Steam Limited

Printed by Tyson Press, Gainsborough House,
81 Oxford St, London, W1D 2EU

Text Copyright © Audrey Kenwrick
Illustrations all rights reserved

Published 2014

The moral right of the author has been asserted.
No part of this publication may be reproduced, stored
in a retrieval system, or transmitted in any form or by
any means, electronic, mechanical, photocopying,
recording or otherwise without permission.

A CIP Catalogue Record for this book is available
from the British Library

ISBN 978-0-9576713-6-2

Contents

Book 1 - Little Chuff and Igor
1 - Little Chuff and Igor 3
2 - Magical Grace & Frank McGregor 10
3 - Laura Doolan 13
4 - Wheels are put in Motion 18
5 - Work commences on Little Chuff 22
6 - The Grand Opening... 25
7 - The First Footplate Experience 28
8 - Little Chuff's Birthday Party Début 32
9 - Naughty Nigel's Birthday Party 42
10 - The End of the Day 47
11 - A Seaside Trip for Igor................................... 48
12 - Very Excited Children on Board 51
13 - Down on the Beach... 55
14 - Homeward Bound.. 58
The bit at the end of the first book..................... 60

Book 2- Imagination World
1 - Grace in Imagination World........................... 63
2 - Fairy Land 73
3 - The Rescue... 80
4 - Tully is Back Home 83
5 - Time to go Home... 89
6 - Happenings on the Journey Home................. 91
7 - Hobgoblins End Station 95
8 - Queen Saffron Retaliates............................... 103
9 - After the Truce 110
10 - Preparation & Arrival into Elfin World ... 112
11 - Jubilant Journey back to Fairy Land 122
12 - Going Home 124
Postscript... 126

Adventures in Steam

By
Rosie Muffett

Book 1
Little Chuff
& Igor

Adventures in Steam

Book 1

Little Chuff and Igor

By
Rosie Muffett

1 - Little Chuff and Igor

The rain was pouring from the darkened skies soaking the spindly branches of the high trees which screened the railway site. Tall Trees Steam Railway Museum was hidden behind the huge poplars which now looked limp and sodden.

Little Chuff listened to the clap of thunder, his eyes rolled in fear as he watched the lightening explode in the skies which eerily lit up the shed where he lived. The rain began to seep over his wheels as it poured under the doors. He shivered, and tears fell from his enormous blue eyes.

This was where disused engines were stored who were no longer any use to the railway. Chuff was a little shunting engine and for years when he was younger he would shunt carriages up and down the tracks. His work was important at the time but now his poor little body was covered in rust and was falling apart. He felt abandoned and was afraid he could be heading for the scrap yard. During night time he lay awake and thought if it wasn't for his friend Igor who lived alongside him in the shed, he would have given up hope a long time ago.

As for Igor, he had been a very busy engine who had been an essential part of the railway pulling carriages on the main lines to other parts of the country. But now, he too was feeling worried about his future and was in need of costly repairs.

However, Igor's new role was to stand as an exhibit in the yard. This was a very boring existence for him as engineers would explain to visitors how a steam engine worked. Igor loved to hear the happy sound of laughter from the children when they were allowed to clamber onto his footplate.

One night, Little Chuff and Igor were awake talking until the wee small hours of the morning discussing their future.

"What do you think is going to happen to us?" said Chuff.

"Dunno" Igor replied, "not sure, but I overheard Mr McGregor talking to a woman the other day,"....

Chuff interrupted Igor; "what has she got to do with us?" he asked.

"Well," Igor went on, "she was saying something about driving steam engine courses for my engine and children having their birthday parties on your carriage."

"Birthday parties....for my engine and carriage....for me....what on earth does she mean, and what else did I hear you say?"
Igor repeated what he had told him.

"The woman is stupid." Chuff said sounding bad tempered.

Igor heard the tone in his friend's voice and decided to ignore it.

"Well," he continued, "she seemed to be concerned about the railway. I think there are new plans afoot for all of us, no matter what you think, but I really don't understand what's going on."

Igor's mouth turned down at the sides and he now looked as tired and miserable as Chuff,

"Anyway," he said, "let's wait and see what tomorrow brings and not worry any more. I think the most important thing is for us to get some sleep." Igor was now aware that Chuff was looking upset about their discussion.

"Mr McGregor will be here soon to lubricate you with some soothing oil for your joints so you won't seize up," he said, "You really are rusted up very badly in some of your working parts, Chuff."

Chuff knew that Igor was his soul mate who cared for him. Without his moral support over the years and Mr McGregor's caring hands, he would have long since been carted away for scrap.

"Thank you for your kind words, what would I do without you?" said the little steam engine as a big tear drop rolled down his tiny fat face.

"I know everything will be all right, I am sure of it, just you wait and see Chuff, things have a way of working themselves out," Igor said, "night night my little friend."

Igor hoped with these few words he had given some assurance to Chuff about the matter, even though he had his doubts.

The next morning Joe and Bill arrived at the shed to examine Chuff and Igor. They were loyal engineers who had spent many years working as volunteers for the steam railway museum. As they began to speak the two engines listened closely to the conversation.

"It's no good," Joe began, "just look at Chuff's body, half of it is covered in rust and it will take a lot of time and money to do the work. The railway has no spare cash so it looks like Chuff will have to be scrapped and the money that brings in will have to pay for Igor's repairs."

Bill nodded in agreement and heaved a sigh of sadness. With a grim look on his face replied to Joe, "I agree with what you are saying. We had better go and report our findings to Frank McGregor and see what he has to say on the matter."

"OK Bill, there is nothing more we can do now for Chuff," Joe said miserably, and on that note, they turned on their heel and left the shed.

When the two engines heard what the engineers had said Chuff began to cry, the tears poured down his face. Igor too was fighting back his tears and knew there was nothing he could say or do that would make his little friend feel better.

Later that night neither of them slept as they wondered when the lorry would come to take Little Chuff away.

Joe and Bill headed for the office to give McGregor their report.

"Sit down.... sit down lads," Frank said, "shall we have a cup of tea?"

As McGregor listened to their tale of woe, the expression on his face changed to one of concern. He was very fond of Little Chuff and could not imagine anything worse than having to send him away to be scrapped. He knew that Grace, his little daughter would be heartbroken if that happened. He looked at the two men,

"You know lads, I've have been wracking my brains trying to think of a solution for weeks.....but unfortunately I haven't come up with anything. In fact I have had sleepless nights over this dilemma."

The two men nodded in agreement and said they felt exactly the same. The meeting came to an end and on that final sad note they said goodbye and left the office.

2 - Magical Grace & Frank McGregor

In spite of money difficulties Mr McGregor, the manager of the museum was determined to find a way to keep the railway open. Recently he had been paying for some of the bills out of his own pocket and he did his best running the railway on a small amount of money. He knew the lack of funds was serious and the situation was getting worse. He wondered how things would turn out.

Mr McGregor and his family lived in a cottage supplied by the railway. His daughter, Grace, saw her favourite engine Little Chuff, every day. Grace had shiny long red hair and large green eyes, but most importantly, she had a kind nature. Her Mother, Maud, was a plump and homely woman. She loved to bake and always had plenty of scones and cakes to offer Grace's friends when they came to tea.

You see children what you don't know is that Grace had a secret. She had magical powers.

Some time ago, one night, she had a dream. In that dream, a fairy told her that Queen Saffron of Fairy Land had chosen her because she was a special little girl. Grace was told that one day soon they would need her help.

From that day on Grace found that she was able to talk to Little Chuff and Igor...but there was one important rule...Grace had to keep this secret close to her heart otherwise the magical powers would stop.

One day, after Grace returned from school, she skipped along humming her favourite song. Arriving at the shed, Chuff smiled when he heard her sweet voice singing.

"You are my sunshine, my only sunshine, you make me happy when skies are grey, you never know dear, how much I love you, please don't take my sunshine away.

Chuff thought to himself with a heavy heart, she always sings this song to me and he wondered how long it would be before he would ever see or hear her again.

"Oh Chuff I do love you," she said as she jumped up on his footplate and plonked a big kiss on his nose.

3 - Laura Doolan

Then one day soon after, Mr McGregor received a phone call from a woman. Her name was Laura Doolan. She said she knew the steam railway had money troubles and reminded him of their previous conversation. At the time Mr McGregor hadn't paid attention, but now he listened eagerly. Laura said she had a plan which might help the railway.

He agreed to meet Laura at his office the following morning, and while he waited for her to arrive he put the kettle on. He wondered what on earth she had to say which could help them out of their troubles.

When Laura arrived and entered the dimly lit office they shook hands and Mr McGregor offered her a cup of tea. As they sipped tea together, Laura began to explain.

"The first plan is for Igor, I'm sure that steam buffs would love to drive a steam engine," she said. "Igor has a big engine and foot plate so he would be perfect for this adventure. The double track means that Igor can be driven down one side and back up the other."

With excitement mounting in her voice she continued, "Your volunteers could work out simple instructions for people to follow." Now smiling broadly, she said, "I'm sure there are many enthusiasts from all over the country who would love to drive a steam engine, Mr McGregor?"

Frank scratched his chin looking at her over the top of his spectacles, "what an absolute brilliant plan, he said, "why hadn't I thought of this before, my only concern would be the issue of health and safety, but I will look into it straight away."

Laura continued to speak saying, "we could have a grand opening and invite newspapers, TV and radio to broadcast the events and invite a celebrity along."

Mr McGregor liked what he heard, and even more, he liked Laura. He knew she was a person that would work happily alongside him at the railway. When she mentioned just how much money could be made he was staggered and realised that it might save the railway from closure.

"My dear I will put your plan to the authorities and let you know as soon as possible. As far as I am concerned the plan has my blessing."

Laura's face beamed and then she went on to tell him about her idea for Little Chuff.

"I'm sure that children would love to have their birthday parties on a moving train, but first we need to change Chuff's image. He will need a carriage attached to his engine big enough to seat thirty-six children."

Mr McGregor thought this was a great idea too and he realised that Laura was a very smart young woman who had thought of everything.

Laura was thrilled at the prospect of working for Tall Trees Railway. The meeting came to an end and as they shook hands and said good-bye, Mr McGregor said "I will call you very soon Laura."

"OK, that will be fine and if you get approval we will call the project, 'Adventures in Steam'."

Later on that week when the plan was presented to the authorities, they gave it their full approval along with their very best wishes for its future success.

Now it was full steam ahead with the plans which began immediately.

4 - Wheels are put in Motion

The rumours soon went round the railway that an agreement had been made with a mystery lady called Laura who had big plans for Tall Trees. That day, Igor was impatient to be brought back to the shed so he could tell Little Chuff what he had heard.

Igor knew he was to have an overhaul to enable footplate experiences to take place on his engine. But there was no confirmation yet regarding the outcome of any changes for Chuff.

A few weeks later the work which had been done on Igor had come to an end and he now looked in pristine condition. His old dull black paintwork was shiny and new. His brass parts had been polished to a dazzling shine. His nameplates and number 971518 had been repainted black on gold and he looked incredible.

In the meantime, poor Chuff had been sleeping a lot during the days as there was nothing for him to stay awake for anyway, he thought grumpily. Igor is hardly ever here now he was thinking to himself and in any case he was so tired by the time he returned at night, the little steam engine was usually fast asleep.

It was early spring when one morning Chuff heard a lot of activity in the top corner of his footplate cabin. He had been aware that a blackbird family had chosen to build their nest there. He suddenly could hear a lot of noisy chirping and it sounded like the baby chicks had hatched. Chuff was delighted as he watched the excited parents flying in and out of the nest feeding their young all day. It made him feel useful. At least the birds need me, he thought sadly these days! Then he suddenly reminded himself that he did not know how many days he had left at the railway which made him feel even more alone than ever. However, his one consoling thought was that his sacrifice would benefit Igor.

When Igor was brought back to the shed later that day, he said, "Hey, are you awake?" Chuff was dozing.

"Of course I am silly, how was your day?" he replied.

Igor was trying to keep the excitement out of his voice and said, "You will not believe this, do you remember that lady who came to see Mr McGregor and I told you they were talking about driving courses....well, guess what? They are planning a grand opening soon and there will be TV cameras and radio here."

Chuff, now looking under his eyes at his excited friend said in a sorrowful voice, "you're all sorted then, I'm happy for you Igor, but I expect they will want me out of the way more than ever now."

Unable to hold back the other good news Igor had any longer, the excitement rising in his voice, replied, "that's not going to happen Chuff, I have just heard they have agreed a plan for you too and it's for children to have their birthday parties in your carriage."

"Birthday parties, birthday parties....what on earth are you babbling on about," he said crossly.

"You're not listening properly," Igor replied, now realising in his haste he had not made it clear what he was trying to say.

"Sorry, I will explain it to you better... it's the excitement of it all you see. Mr McGregor said that the parties will be for children up to the age of ten. They are painting your body in bright orange with black stripes down each side and the work starts tomorrow... how's that?"

Chuff struggled to take it all in and said, "I can hardly believe my luck, oh Igor, I'm so happy," he replied. Little Chuff began to cry with happiness and Igor just grinned.

Needless to say they both slept peacefully that night thinking of the exciting future which now lay ahead for them both.

5 - Work commences on Little Chuff

Early next morning there was great activity in the shed. Joe and Bill arrived armed with the necessary equipment ready to start work on Chuff. They began to scrape the rust off Chuff's engine using a wire brush. The grinding and hammering continued all day and every day for ten days. Chuff's body ached, but finally when they put the red lead paint all over his engine it soothed his little body.

Igor was very kind as usual, and he would tell his friend funny stories to take his mind off all the work being done. One night, soon after, Igor said with excitement in his voice,

"It will be over soon and you will be the best looking engine here. Just YOU think of that."

These kind words helped Chuff to be patient. He knew Igor was right and soon the day dawned when the work was finished. Chuff looked all shiny and new and his engine had been checked and found to be in good order, thanks to Frank McGregor.

Grace watched every day and her heart raced with delight at the changes taking place at Tall Trees Railway. Her eyes opened wide with amazement when she finally saw Little Chuff. He was now the colour of an orange. His big dark blue eyes peering out looked even bigger than before. Black stripes marched down the sides of his engine and the first-class carriage to which he was coupled. The interior of the carriage had six tables in total, three each side of the carriage. Each table could seat six children, and the seats were squishy and comfortable. They were covered in a soft striped navy blue and yellow velvet material.

As Grace gazed in wonderment at the scene she said, "Oh my friend, how really incredible you look.... you now look ready to party."

Grace's 7th birthday was the following week. Giggling and laughing at an idea she had thought of, she wondered if she would be allowed to have her birthday party on Little Chuff's carriage. With this idea in mind she promptly ran off to ask if it was possible. As she entered the office she said "Excuse me Daddy can I have my birthday party on Chuff."

Mr McGregor put his pen down and looked at his little girl replying,

"I will speak to Laura and if she thinks it's a good idea it could be a good trial run for the parties."

Grace put her arms around him and thanked him as she merrily ran off to tell Chuff. Now thinking to herself, wait till Chuff hears that I might be allowed to have my party on his carriage... with a bit of luck.

6 - The Grand Opening

The railway was now making progress and the bookings for both the footplate experiences and birthday parties were coming in fast. On the day of the grand opening a local brass band had kindly offered to play. That Sunday was a warm and sunny day, and when Little Chuff emerged from the shed he could not believe his eyes. His face lit up as he struggled to hold back tears of happiness.

The railway looked spectacular. It had been painted and tidied, coloured bunting decorated the whole area. There were TV cameras televising the event live and local radio broadcasting on air.

Then, to the sound of fanfare the Lord Mayor arrived. As he stepped up on the stage he announced how happy he was to see the wonderful changes that had been made. He congratulated everyone who had been involved in all the hard work which had been done. And then, Scarlet, the local carnival queen appeared, she was tall and very pretty with long fair hair and wore her crown with pride.

As she cut the ribbon to open the event, everyone cheered as the happy onlookers clapped and the Lord Mayor announced:

"Adventures in Steam"....is now open for business"

When he finished his speech, the band began to play, and people were smiling and laughing with happiness as the children danced round and round to the music.

"What a sight to behold," said Igor to Chuff as they looked on thrilled at the wonderful scene before them.

When the day's events came to a close, Igor looked forward to the next day when the first footplate experience was due to start.

Later on that night when they were back in the shed, Igor said to Chuff,

"Night night, sweet dreams" and Chuff sleepily replied, "You too my friend" as they promptly fell sleep, both with a big smile on their faces.

7 - The First Footplate Experience

Igor woke up early the next morning, he was breathless with excitement and shouted across to Chuff,

"Hey wake up, this is my big day, I can't wait to get out on the tracks."

"It's really exciting for you, I wish you all the luck in the world," his friend replied. "Have a great day and I'll look forward to seeing you when you come back, you can tell me all about it then."

It was six am in the morning when Joe and Bill arrived saying it was a bright and sunny day. A crowd had already gathered alongside the track waiting to watch the first footplate experience.

When the first customer arrived, Joe introduced himself to the elderly gentleman.

"Good morning, my name is Joe, and you must be Clive," he said, as they shook hands. The man replied,

"I am very excited at the prospect of driving Igor, it's a retirement gift bought for me by my wife... this is a dream come true."

"How wonderful for you" Joe said, "we will make sure that you have an unforgettable day, Clive."

He then took Clive into the waiting room and handed him a health and safety document to read.

"This is essential reading before you can drive a steam engine."

Then handing him overalls provided by the railway to change into, he said "driving a steam engine can be a hot, dirty and dusty experience."

When they boarded the foot plate, Clive and Joe shovelled coal onto the fire until it was red hot. This built such a head of steam in the boiler that the safety valve on top released a great hissing noise which frightened the onlookers. With a sudden jerk as Clive released the hand brake, the big engine slowly started to move down the track. As Igor chugged his way out of the station a loud whistle could be heard which was deafening.

The engine was gathering pace along the four mile track and Igor felt very proud, thinking to himself at long last I am needed again.

When he reached the end of the track there was a large turn-table which Clive and Joe had to manoeuvre Igor on to. There were a few volunteers waiting to help. The train had to be turned around to enable it to head down the opposite side of the track and back to the station. The instructions were loud and clear from Tom and the turntable crew,

"Around to the left, a little to the right," and then the wheels were linked up facing back down the track.

The exercise was completed in no time at all, and Joe and Clive shovelled more coal on to the fire. Then with a loud whistle blast, Igor started to move again.

Clive took the controls and drove the engine back to the station where the cheering crowd was waiting on the platform to see their safe return.

When Igor finally appeared puffing and huffing round the bend, another loud shriek from the whistle rang out much to the delighted looks on the people's faces. Then the engine was put in reverse and they set off backwards. The trip was repeated again, including braking and flat out speed much to the pleasure of Clive.

When Clive's adventure had come to an end, it was over far too quickly as far as he was concerned. He had enjoyed driving Igor very much. So with his face as black as coal and a big grin, he promptly headed straight to the office to book again for another day.

Then Igor rested up for a while, and the next eager driver soon arrived. The footplate experiences continued all day and Igor thought what a brilliant day it all had been.

8 - Little Chuff's Birthday Party Début

Mr McGregor and Laura had agreed that Grace could have her 7th birthday party on Little Chuff the following week. The arrangements were made and with great excitement Grace invited her friends.

The following Saturday on the day of Grace's birthday all her friends arrived at the railway armed with gifts. Willy Willoby, a volunteer at the railway had been specially chosen to host the parties. When the children arrived he handed each of them a yellow and navy blue flag. Then to the sound of drums and waving his large flag, he laughingly shouted,

"Forward march now children, off we go on our adventure."

Willy Willoby, a rather large gentleman, with a big personality, spent some of his spare time volunteering to drive disabled children in his car twice a year to a seaside resort. He was well thought of especially by the children whom he had grown to love. Willy had a long grey beard and wore a white shirt with a black waistcoat over it. He was unable to do the buttons up because of his big fat tummy which shook like a jelly when he walked.

His huge baggy black trousers and big black boots he wore made him look a little like a clown. On his head he wore a large yellow hat shaped like a flying saucer which wobbled around.

Flynn, Grace's friend, was staring at Mr Willoby's hat and said quite indignantly, "that's not a proper train guard's hat," and he replied,

"No, I know... but it's much funnier isn't it Flynn?"

Flynn nodded in agreement grinning broadly while the children boarded the train listening to funny Mr Willoby shouting "all aboard, all aboard" waving his flag in the air.

Peals of laughter could be heard as each child sat down in their seats waiting for the train to move. Then a loud whistle was heard and a great hissing sound from the engine as Little Chuff slowly began to move away from the platform on its journey. The children cheered with delight and waving their flags shouted goodbye to their parents. "See you all later" they said. Little Chuff felt a surge of pride as he headed off with his happy party goers on his first exciting journey.

Clackety-clack, clackety-clack, could be heard as the little engine picked up speed heading down the track.

Inside the carriage the tables were covered in yellow crepe paper. Each table had small pots of yellow daffodils placed in the centre. The birthday cake made of mouth-watering sponge with butter cream and raspberry jam inside stood high on a separate table. The icing was white and decorated around the top and bottom were pink and white roses. In the centre of the cake stood seven pink candles. "Oohs" and "ahhs" could be heard from the children, "can we have a piece now please?".... little Kate asked, and the rest nodded in agreement and Mr Willoby said, "you will have to be patient children and wait a little while longer."

When the train moved out of the station, Mr Willoby handed each child a gaily coloured cardboard box. The box had a picture of Little

Chuff smiling on the front. Inside there was a selection of mouth-watering goodies.

As the children opened their boxes, Elizabeth said,

"Oh look all my favourite things to eat; we have finger sandwiches with cheese and ham, crisps, a cup cake, jelly and chocolate fingers,"

"Wow," said Logan, a blond tousled haired classmate,

"I'm starving, let's get stuck in then," piped up his mischievous little brother, Flynn, and as they began to tuck into their feast Chuff began to pick up speed.

When they reached the end of the railway line and the party food had been eaten, Mr Willoby announced that the next part of the journey would be especially interesting for them.

"Please children all stand up and look out of the windows."

He explained that the train had to be turned around on the turntable in order for them to travel back down the track. The children watched with great curiosity as they had never seen anything like this before. The crew who were on hand to help were very helpful and soon the operation was safely completed.

Finally, Chuff was ready to take the children back to the station and Mr Willoby announced,

"Before we head back children, we are going to light the candles on Grace's birthday cake."

They all chorused, "Yippee," now gathering around Grace and singing loudly, *"Happy birthday to you, happy birthday to you, happy birthday dear Grace, happy birthday to you."*

Then Mr Willoby said, "Three cheers for Grace, hip, hip hurray, hip, hip hurray, hip, hip hurray."

They all sat down again and Chuff was ready to be driven back to the station by Joe. A big cheer went up as the orange train slowly started to chug its way back down the track. Suddenly, Logan, realising that Flynn was no longer sitting next to him yelled out anxiously,

"Mr Willoby, Mr Willoby, where's Flynn?"

"What?" he shouted, "what do you mean, where's Flynn?"

"Well he was here a minute ago" Logan said.

After searching the carriage and looking under the seats, Mr Willoby pulled the communication cord and Joe, the engine driver, stopped the train,

"What's up Mr Willoby," Joe shouted as he climbed aboard the carriage.

"We have one child missing and his name is Flynn."

"Right," said Joe, "everyone sit down and I will back the train up and we'll put out a search party for him, don't worry Logan we will find him."

Joe then had a thought and said,

"The only place we stopped where Flynn could have sneaked off the train was at the turntable when I opened the back door of the carriage to talk to you Mr Willoby, perhaps that's what happened."

Logan and Flynn were very close brothers and poor Logan feeling upset said,

"But he was right by my side when we were singing happy birthday to Grace." And Mr Willoby nodded,

"I saw him too I wonder where he went to?"

When Chuff pulled onto the turntable, Mr Willoby said,

"We have to split into two search parties, Joe you take this group and I will take the rest."

As the two groups headed into the bluebell woods nearby Mr Willoby bellowed,

"Joe you go that way and we will go the other."

As they proceeded to go in different directions Grace began to cry.

"What if we cannot find him." she said.

"Don't be silly, I am sure there is a simple explanation to this and he will suddenly turn up, he can't have gone that far," Mr Willoby said.

After searching the woods there was no sign of Flynn anywhere. Mr Willoby then made a decision to head back to the main station to get help.

With downturned mouths the children boarded the train and Logan said,

"What's that noise Mr Willoby,"

"Be quiet everyone....listen." he replied

Suddenly, they all realised that the noise was coming from the toilet, and as Mr Willoby opened the door everyone burst out laughing. Flynn was sitting on the toilet fast asleep, and when he opened his eyes he could not understand what all the fuss was about.

"Right" said Mr Willoby, "everyone sit back down as I am late for the next party and your parents will be wondering where we are."

Mr Willoby was happy thinking to himself, I am so glad that little Flynn was found safe and well.

Chuff headed back to the main station and Mr Willoby began to sing and all the children joined in,

"If you're happy and you know it clap your hands. If you're happy and you know it clap your hands, if you're happy and you know it, don't forget to show it, if you're happy and you know it clap your hands."

Very soon they pulled into Tall Trees Station where all the parents were waiting and the excited children were eager to tell them about their adventure.

Later that night as Grace climbed into her comfy bed. She giggled thinking to herself how silly they all had been not looking in the toilet for Flynn in the first place!

What a lovely day I have had, she thought, I wonder what tomorrow will bring? Settling down for the night, she smiled as she fell fast asleep.

9 - Naughty Nigel's Birthday Party

Mr Willoby gazed ahead and saw Nigel and his party all waiting for him to take them on their trip. The boys were all dressed up and eerily looked like trolls. With their long white beards and pointed noses they did indeed look quite frightening. Oh well he thought to himself, boys will be boys. There were twenty in total, and as he marched them off to board Chuff he had a feeling that this was going to be a party with a few problems!

When the train pulled out of the station some of the boys refused to sit down at the tables. When the boxes of food were handed out a few started to throw the food at one another.

Poor Mr Willoby didn't know what to do. He was faced with chaos, the lads were ruffians. They were running up and down the corridor smearing chocolate on the windows and spilling drinks all over the floor slipping about and falling all over the place.

Then much to Mr Willoby's horror, naughty Nigel and horrible Harry grabbed the birthday cake and threw it straight into his face!

The cream, jam and icing slithered down his nose and dripped all over his clean shirt and onto the floor. The poor man slipped on the mess and went "Crash Bang Wallop." The boys were holding their tummies laughing out loud and pointing their fingers at him as Mr Willoby rolled round on the floor struggling to get to his feet.

Mr Willoby was furious and pulled the communication cord to get help from Joe.

Chuff came to a screeching halt and as Joe and Fred boarded the carriage they could not believe their eyes when they saw the mess.

"Right," Joe shouted, "you lot....you'll immediately apologise to Mr Willoby and start to clean the place up straight away,.... your party," now addressing Nigel, "is over and as soon as you have cleared up we will head back and inform your parents."

The boys all hung their heads in shame realising that they had spoilt all the fun they could have had and were now heading for deep trouble.

When the train arrived back at the station and Igor heard all about the goings on, he knew that if he had any say in the matter those boys would be banned forever from the railway.

The parents came forward to collect their children. They wondered what on earth was going on when the boys were frog marched immediately to Mr McGregor's office. On hearing about their disgraceful behaviour they were all banned officially from ever having another birthday party at the railway again. Needless to say apologies were extended and their punishment was well deserved.

Back at the office, Mr Willoby who was now feeling very tired after the day sat down to a welcome cup of tea made by Grace. She simply shook her head as she handed him a much needed cuppa. After he changed out of his smeared stained clothing, Grace put them in a bag saying she would get them cleaned assuring him she would bring them back looking like new in no time at all.

"Oh well Mr Willoby," she said, "I expect these things will happen occasionally, but the boys cleaned up the mess and are very sorry for all the trouble they caused you know."

"I expect so," he said, heaving a sigh and closing his eyes, promptly fell asleep.

Grace smiled as she covered him with a blanket and crept out of the office leaving poor Mr Willoby to recover.

10 - The End of the Day

When the day came to a very exciting end, Grace hugged her Daddy saying,

"That was a great party, thank you so much, but I must go and thank Chuff."

Making her way to see her friend, she said, "Goodnight and thank you Chuff so much for making my birthday party the best ever, see you both tomorrow, night night, sweet dreams, I love you both."

As she turned on her heel and left the shed Igor grinned and said to Chuff,

"I told you things would be all right,"

Chuff smiled and winked saying, "yes our Guardian Angel was certainly looking after us."

And on that note, both friends fell fast asleep happy and contented looking forward to the next day's adventures.

11 - A Seaside Trip for Igor

The following week Laura called a meeting with Frank McGregor to discuss another idea she had been thinking of for the railway. She knew the authorities would have to agree and as they sat down together sipping their tea, Laura began to chat.

"Would it be possible to arrange an excursion to the seaside, I was thinking we could travel to Weston-Super-Mare and use Igor for the trip, what do you think?"

"That sounds brilliant," he enthused, and she continued to say,

"We could schedule this outing to take place during the school holidays and it would include several stops en route. I also want to tell you about a local orphanage."

"Oh," he said,

"The Dovecote Orphanage is owned by Olive Bayliss, and I know most of the children who live there have never been to the seaside. I thought it would be a generous thing for you to offer free tickets for them to come on the excursion?"

Mr McGregor fingered his chin, "yes I agree, I will get back to you as soon as possible and let you know."

"Thank you Mr McGregor," she replied, "I'll look forward to hearing from you," waving goodbye as she went.

Laura went to visit the Orphanage and introduced herself as she felt sure the excursion would take place during the summer. The Dovecote Orphanage was for children who had been abandoned through different circumstances. Some of them had been left on doorsteps just after they were born and their parents had never been found, and a few children had been taken away from bad parents.

As Mrs Bayliss and Laura sat down she told her about her idea.

"That all sounds wonderful. We would be delighted to accept your kind invitation and I will wait to hear from you."

Soon after the meeting permission was granted. It was now full steam ahead for Laura who would organise the excursion.

12 - Very Excited Children on Board

The day soon dawned for the outing which was a bright and sunny day, and as Igor stood proudly with steam hissing and smoke pouring from his engine, he was impatiently waiting to set off for the day at the seaside. Grace, and her Mum, Maud, were among the happy travellers.

The children from the Orphanage arrived early at the steam railway and eagerly clambered on board. They sat down in their specially reserved seats. On the tables were lemonade and sweets which Mr McGregor had very kindly provided. Mrs Bayliss knew this was the very first time for the children to have visited the seaside and she was so grateful to the railway for providing the outing.

"How kind of them to give us these goodies as well," she said, "isn't it great, we will soon be on our way."

With a shrill blast from the whistle and Igor's drive wheels spinning and squealing on the track, he set off to the sounds of cheers from the children. Igor passed through unscheduled stops and the passengers saw lots of people lining the platforms waving flags. When they pulled into the scheduled stops to allow new ticket holders on board, the train was full to overflowing.

Igor was now travelling high up along the edge of the coastal track at great speed. When suddenly, and without warning, a wild deer ran across in front of the train. Igor's engine braked furiously, the train juddered and shuddered and skidded along the track, the children clung on to their seats.

Grace could feel the wheels of the train beginning to leave the track. There was a cliff on one side of the train, she knew that only she could help and didn't have long. She closed her eyes and concentrated hard; she imagined the wheels of the train safely back on the track...sure enough, in a few seconds the bumping and shuddering reduced.

The train slowed to a stop safely on the track. The passengers all cheered with relief. "That was a close shave," thought Grace, she had never used her powers to stop a steam train before! Then everyone settled down again for the rest of the journey.

Grace began to wonder if this was the reason why she had been given magical powers. What Grace didn't know was that she would need to use her powers more than she could imagine for all the dangerous and exciting adventures in store for her and Little Chuff.

When all the excitement had died down, and everyone felt safe, Igor drove through the last tunnel to get to its destination. The sea could be seen glistening in the bright sunshine. The seagulls could be heard squawking as they flew overhead flapping their white wings.

At this point all the orphans bursting with excitement began to sing:

"*I see the sea, I see the sea.*"

When they arrived at the station Grace went to see if Igor was alright; derailing can't be nice for an engine. But before she could say anything Igor said,

"Thank you Grace, I knew that was you. You saved us all." Grace felt very proud.

13 - Down on the Beach

An enthralled group of children arrived on the beach that day. As each of them began to undress they raced towards the sea for a swim all shouting in delight, "this is great fun, please can we come here again Mrs Bayliss?"

A picnic lunch was provided and the delighted band of children sat in a circle tucking into their feast. In their lunch boxes they had a variety of sandwiches, sausage rolls, crisps, cupcakes, apples, oranges and lemonade to drink. As they hungrily ate their delicious food the sounds of: "Yummy, yummy," could be heard. Soon after a few of the girls played ball games in the sand. Others just walked towards the sea enjoying watching the rest of them play.

Some of the children were invited to join in and had a great time making new friends. A few addresses were exchanged and promises made to keep in touch.

By now it was getting late and Mrs Bayliss said,

"I know you don't want to go but I have decided that we will return every year."

As she rounded them up for their return journey, the children all whooped with delight when they heard this. They could not believe their luck.

They were happy now at the thought of the journey on the steam train home knowing they would be coming back one day soon.

On returning to the Orphanage, Mrs Bayliss rang Mr McGregor. She told him the Orphanage would fund the trip to the seaside every year from now on.

14 - Homeward Bound

Back at Weston-Super-Mare Station, Joe, could not find Fred, the fireman who stoked the engine anywhere.

"Oh dear," said Joe, "now what can I do?"

Word quickly went round the train there was a problem and they were a man short on the footplate.

As luck would have it, Clive, who had been one of the first people to experience a driving course at the railway, was on board. He ran to the footplate calling out to Joe.

"Hey Joe, remember me, can I help?"

"Of course Clive, that would be great, hop up and put Fred's overalls on and let's get going."

As soon as Clive got on board they headed off. Several hours later they arrived safely back to Tall Trees Station.

Finally, at the end of an exhausting but fulfilling day, Igor and Little Chuff were chatting about the happenings and how brilliantly everything had turned out, especially because of Grace's magical powers.

Little Chuff and Igor then both fell asleep happily dreaming of what adventures tomorrow would bring.

---The End---

The bit at the end of the first book

Here is a puzzle for you to work out. See how long it will take you to figure out how Igor got his number 971518!

Here is a clue: Look at the alphabet.

Adventures in Steam

By
Rosie Muffett

Book 2
Imagination
World

Adventures in Steam
Book 2

Imagination World

By
Rosie Muffett

1 - Grace in Imagination World

Grace woke up with a start. She stared into the faces of two little creatures who were jumping up and down like clowns on her bed. They were making such a racket. I must be dreaming she thought, and pinching herself realized she was awake. Feeling a little scared,

"Who are you?" she said.

"We are trolls and our names are Honk and Gonk" they chorused. "We won't hurt you Grace but we need your help desperately."

The odd pair looked at her with wide eyes and for some reason she no longer felt afraid. In fact she thought they were rather sweet in spite of their strange appearance.

"OK" she replied, and now leaping out of bed and curious to hear what they had to say she bent down to listen.

"Speak up," said Grace, wondering what gobble de gook she would hear.

"You must come with us," they implored, "you and Little Chuff, hurry."

It was a cold wintry night and the wind was howling rustling the trees which surrounded the railway. Grace put her warm coat on over her jimjams. As the three of them hurried towards the shed with the trolls in hot pursuit, she began to wonder what Little Chuff would have to say when he saw them.

"It's all right Chuff," she shouted, "Sorry to wake you in the middle of the night but these are my two friends who have something to ask us, their names are Honk and Gonk."

Honk and Gonk, what silly names, he thought. Honk, the leader of the two began to explain to Chuff.

"We are friendly trolls who have been banished along with a few others by King Snotty of Hobgoblins Village on the dark side of the mountain, he said. "We now live on the other side with Queen Saffron in Fairy Land."

"Yes," said Gonk joining in, "we love the pixies, fairies and gnomes who live there. They are very kind and allow us to share their houses with them, but our Queen needs help. Will you and Chuff come with us to Fairy Land please?"

Grace wondered what Fairy Land would be like. She felt butterflies in her tummy at the thought of going there.

"Oh please, please Chuff," she said, "let's go with them to Fairy Land."

Grace noticed that Honk and Gonk had big conks. Honk had a long white beard and he was bigger than his friend Gonk and stood about 25cm tall. He had a big fat bottom and large dewy blue eyes and his huge ears flapped in the breeze.

His feet were fat and enormous and when he walked it looked as if he was following them, and he wore no shoes. His hair, a mixture of colours, matted badly and smelt fusty and horrid.

When he smiled half of his teeth were missing. But the expression he wore was one of kindness. His blue faded dungarees and jacket were shabby and old. As for Gonk, he was much tinier in stature. His arms were folded over his huge tummy which burst out over his purple trousers. His eyes, the colour of emerald green were set close together. His feet and ears were very large, but not as big as Honks, but he too had teeth missing when he smiled. His wispy bit of pink hair stuck out from under his cap which was perched on top of his head. But when he smiled with a toothless grin, Grace thought his smile could light up a room.

Honk had another big problem, his tail, it was long, fat, and hairy and in order to stop it trailing behind him he had to wrap it around his body. Sometimes he would forget and then the poor thing would constantly trip and bump into things. This made life very uncomfortable for all the male trolls to sit down, other than on a toad stool. They were born with these tails you see and it made them very grumpy.

Honk could be heard saying out loud, "oh bother me tail please go away." All the trolls thought their tails were a nuisance, but the female's tails were not as long. They all had another problem....their noses! They stuck out from their faces such a long way. As you can imagine this caused them to walk into things and at times each other! They often wished they hadn't been born with them and hoped one day something could happen to make their tails and noses shorter.

They were an odd looking pair, and Little Chuff having been rudely awoken gazed with bleary eyes at the two strangers. He managed to suppress laughing out loud but had to grin.

Chuff liked them and nodding to Grace agreed,

"Ok, let's go, where to?"

"Fairy Land of course Chuff," Grace said.

As they boarded the footplate and Grace shovelled the coal onto the fire the steam began to build up. And as she slowly released the brake lever the engine headed off down the track.

Very soon they came to some points in the track which Grace had never seen before. Suddenly, the train veered off through a gap in the hedge and Grace shouted,

"Hey Chuff we are on a narrower track which appears to be getting smaller and smaller, what's happening?" she said, sounding alarmed,

"I don't know Grace, don't worry we will soon find out."

Just then another really weird thing happened!

Grace and Little Chuff began to shrink. Grace became exactly the same size as the two trolls and Chuff's engine shrank too and now he fitted the track perfectly. They both began to giggle and agreed they quite liked the feeling of being tiny it was amazing.

"I wonder what will happen next," said Grace.

Grace spoke too soon because without any warning, a sudden gust of icy cold wind engulfed them followed by a flurry of tiny snowflakes falling from the skies resembling diamonds tumbling from the heavens. The snow began to cover the little engine which rocked from side to side. It felt like a boat on the ocean waves about to sink.

"Hang on tight Grace," Chuff bellowed, as the engine skidded to a halt.

"Now what," said Grace, shaking with fear. As she looked round she saw Honk lying on the floor with Gonk on top of him and their tails and noses entangled. They were grumping and clumsily trying to break free from one another. Dazed and dizzy Grace helped them to their feet and Honk mumbled,

"We have hit a snow storm it will soon be over don't worry," he said, "at this time of year the weather can be severe one minute and change the next."

But Chuff's engine was stuck in a high drift and the snow was coming down even faster than ever before. He couldn't move one way or the other. Grace began to fret and panicking said,

"What will happen if we are completely covered in snow?" She frantically gripped the side trying to hold on and Chuff bellowed,

"Sound my whistle Grace, "maybe help will arrive from somewhere."

Miraculously the snow suddenly stopped as quickly as it had begun, and Grace said it was as if someone had turned the tap off! The high drift they were stuck in began to melt helped by the heat from the engine's boiler enabling them to move again.

Grace and Chuff heaved a sigh of relief.

"That was close Honk," she said, "I do hope we don't have any more mishaps like that."

"I hope not, that WAS scary," he replied.

"Look ahead you two, it's the tunnel we'll soon be there, I told you we would be all right," Honk shouted.

Grace was shivering and Honk took his old jacket off and put it around her shoulders,

"Thank you so much," and then she shouted to Chuff, "Yippee we will be in Fairy Land soon."

Soon after their ordeal they drove into a tunnel which looked foreboding. It was very dark and in the distance they could see a dazzling light.

2 - Fairy Land

When Chuff came to the end of the tunnel they were suddenly engulfed in a golden magical world of brightness.

"Everything is the colour of gold, even the tracks," Grace said to Chuff in astonishment, "and the station building looks solid gold."

"I wonder if it is REAL gold, if it is these people must be very rich," he replied.

"I'm scared... are you Chuff, and who are all these strange looking creatures standing at the station?" she said.

"I'm frightened too, but there is no turning back now," he replied. Just then Honk shouted,

"Pull into the station, Chuff."

The sign ahead was printed in large gold letters and read:

IMAGINATION WORLD

Grace and Little Chuff began to laugh when they saw the pixies, fairies and gnomes standing there. The others looked just like Honk and Gonk with their long tails and noses. The creatures were all happily waving their golden flags to welcome them. Honk began to explain that Queen Saffron was due to arrive any minute and they were all anxiously waiting to hear what she had to say.

"I know there is trouble afoot," he said, "but don't be frightened, the Queen is very kind and caring and she will explain why we have been summoned to bring you here and to ask for help."

Chuff came to a shuddering halt, and the pixies with their pointed noses and ears and brightly coloured outfits began to dance to the sound of drums in the distance. The fairies, dressed in shimmering dresses of gold and silver waved their wands and were flying around like busy bees cheering their heads off. The gnomes sat on their toadstools smiling broadly dressed in a variety of bright colours. The bells on their quirky red hats tinkled every time they moved.

It was a spectacular scene and now Grace and Chuff began to smile and no longer felt afraid, just excited.

Then the sound of trumpets rang out as the Queen emerged from her castle in a carriage made of gold. It had two large golden wheels which came to a screeching halt.

The two foxes proudly pulling the carriage were called Frolic and Frixie and they were both adorned with collars richly studded with gold. Queen Saffron had a skulk of foxes they were her special pets and she loved their beautiful faces.

Frolic, the mischievous one, looking for attention, decided to cock his leg over the wheel of her gold carriage splashing some of the spectators who stood nearby!

"Hey you," said Frixie somewhat crossly, "you have just wet me and a few others; how rude you are."

The Queen was furious at his behaviour especially in front of visitors, and said to him in a cross voice,

"I will deal with you later," Frolic stuck out his tongue at her and the crowd giggled.

When the Queen stepped down from her carriage and began to speak there was a hushed silence.

"My people," she began, "firstly we must welcome Grace and Little Chuff who have made the perilous journey to help us."

And the crowd all cheered.

"Furthermore," she went on, "as you know we are at war with King Snotty and the hobgoblins and most of the trolls who joined forces with them. But now they have stolen Tully, our beloved train."

The crowd began to boo and shout.

"Silence!" she shouted, and once again a respectful quietness descended upon them as they listened to her every word.

"They have blocked the tunnel to their side of the mountain. We need to clear it before we can rescue Tully with the help of Grace and Little Chuff."

The crowd all cheered, and now the Queen addressing Grace and Chuff said,

"If you both agree, the plan is that Grace will use her powers of imagination to silence your noisy engine Chuff. This will enable you to sneak through the tunnel in the dead of night into their territory while our enemies are asleep and you can rescue Tully."

"I don't know what you mean by the power of my imagination," Grace said. And the Queen replied,

"It is your imagination that has created imagination world and all the creatures in it. That is what gives you power," she said.

"I see," said Grace "but there is something else that puzzles me your highness, will you answer a very important question, it has nothing to do with the rescue,"

"Of course my child, what is it? Speak up, speak up,"

Grace replied, "Why do your fairies collect our teeth from under our pillows when they fall out?

"As you can see, said the Queen, "gold is everywhere here and children's teeth are rare and worth a fortune in imagination world so we use them as money to trade with"

"Oh I see," said Grace, now I understand."

The Queen then said,

"Let us now think about Tully, do you agree to the plan?"

"Yes, your Highness," said Grace, and Chuff nodded.

A huge burst of applause came from the crowd and everyone began to whistle and cheer. And the drums began to thump out loud and clear in a defiant sound.

3 - The Rescue

During that night in the pitch black Grace and Little Chuff headed off towards the other side of the mountain. The inhabitants of the village had toiled all day clearing the tunnel to enable the rescue operation to take place. A new exciting adventure was about to begin for them. Slowly, little by little they neared Hobgoblins End Station and the sound of loud snoring could be heard from the trolls and hobgoblins. Grace began to giggle and Chuff said,

"Hush Grace, we must be quiet."

When they pulled into the station they immediately spotted Tully. Standing all alone at the far end of the track stood Tully looking very miserable. As they approached him Chuff whispered,

"Be very quiet Tully, we are here to rescue you under the Queen's orders, but we must act quickly."

Poor Tully's eyes lit up when he heard Chuff's voice and he smiled broadly.

"Let's get to work now and couple you to Chuff as fast as we can." Grace said.

Tully began to tremble and whimpered softly as the tears rolled down his sad forlorn face,

"I didn't think this was possible I thought I would never see my home again; please get me back to where I belong."

"Of course we will," Chuff replied, "stop crying now hold tight, relax and away we go."

The two engines pulled out of the station in silence, and the fairies flying overhead waved their wands and smiled with relief.

Tully had not been treated at all well by the trolls and hobgoblins, the rust on his body was very painful and his engine was sluggish. He knew before long he would have been discarded in a heap along with the rest of the other engines he saw rotting in the yard. Chuff continued on the journey with tearful Tully safely tucked behind him and the fairies overhead reassuring him by quietly whispering,

"Don't worry Tully; we will have you back home in no time at all." When Chuff chugged into Imagination World Station, Tully felt elated and gave out a sigh of happiness. Now exhausted, they put him safely back in his shed and he promptly fell into a peaceful sleep.

4 - Tully is Back Home

The next morning the sun was shining in Fairy Town. As the crowds gathered to welcome Tully home the sound of drums could be heard beating in the background, Rump a tump tump ...Rump a tump tump. The Queen immediately called her people to gather in the town square and began to speak.

"My good people," she said, "we must firstly thank Grace and Little Chuff for bringing our Tully back to us safe and sound; three cheers for Grace and Little Chuff,"

"Hip hip hurray, hip hip hurray, hip hip hurray." The people danced with happiness but not for long because the Queen said,

"I'm sure you know there will be retaliation from the enemy."

Suddenly, they heard a loud rumbling noise. And when they looked towards the mountain hundreds of trolls and hobgoblins armed with clubs and chanting, "Revenge" "Revenge," were marching down towards the town.

"I knew this would happen," the Queen said looking frightened. Many fled in terror back to their homes. Grace shouted to the Queen,

"Quickly use your spells to stop them," and she replied,

"Our magic doesn't work against other creatures in imagination world and that's YOUR fault!"

"My fault, what do you mean? I don't understand," Grace said sounding indignant.

"Well," said the Queen, in your mind you imagine all trolls and hobgoblins are evil, but if you think of them differently they will change and only you can make it happen."

"Oh, I see," said Grace, "you mean I should imagine that the trolls and hobgoblins are friendly creatures and then they will join your side and everything will be all right again!"

"That's right," the Queen replied.

Grace knew the Queen was right as far as the trolls were concerned, but she knew that no child could EVER think of hobgoblins as anything other than evil, thieving, sneaky and ugly beings.

The armies were advancing thundering down the mountainside with great speed. Grace quickly closed her eyes and thought deeply in her mind imagining they were all friends again. Suddenly, the menacing armies halted and the trolls had stopped and turned in their tracks. The villagers could hear a fierce battle taking place and the noise was deafening as the powerful trolls forced the hobgoblins to retreat. The hobgoblins were seen running like cowards defeated and heading back to their village. One of the older gnomes whose name was Goo, decided to do a "moony" towards the hobgoblins which made the villagers howl with laughter.

Soon after all went quiet and the trolls came running down the mountain side towards the town square. They were crashing into each other with their long noses and tripping over their long tails. But now they were all cheering happily and throwing their clubs in the air shouting, "Yippee, hurrah, hurrah we are coming home, we are coming home."

The villagers emerged from their houses and were no longer afraid. One by one they came to see what was happening and looked on in glee. Their long lost friends were home at last. They were shocked but happy at the scene and wondered how on earth this had happened. The Queen smiled and hugged Grace,

"You did it," she said, "I knew you would, but you WERE right about the hobgoblins."

Grace was amazed at the transformation which had taken place in front of her eyes. She knew it was time to leave but there was something else she needed to do before leaving Fairy Land. And closing her eyes once again she used her powers of imagination to change the tails and noses of all the poor trolls. When she opened them she saw a wonderful sight. To her delight all of the trolls no longer had their long gangly tails and big conks. They were much shorter. Cheers, clapping and sighs of relief were heard as Honk and Gonk gathered all the trolls together to thank Grace. They knew their lives would be much more comfortable now and they all began to sing to her:

"She can do magic, magic, she can do magic, magic, we love you Grace."

Grace smiled and laughed out loud seeing the happiness on the faces of her new found friends. And she knew her good deeds for the day were done.

5 - Time to go Home

There was a big party that night in the town square. The smell of burning logs from the huge bonfire which could be seen for miles around pervaded the village. Everyone was dancing together to the joyful music played by pixie musicians. The unmistakable delicious smell of BBQ sausages filled the air. Plates of the pixies and fairies home baked cup cakes with red and green icing were handed round for all to share. Grace and Chuff smiled as they looked on at the happy band of people. They knew that everything for now would be fine. They had done what Queen Saffron, Honk and Gonk wanted them to do, but now it was time to head home.

Next morning, Chuff was waiting at the station bedecked in flags and surrounded by serious looking trolls who were guarding him. The entire population and Tully were there to bid them a sad farewell. Lots of tears were shed especially by Honk and Gonk. Just then the drums began to roll and Queen Saffron arrived in her carriage. As she stepped down with a beaming smile on her face, she said,

"you are welcome here any time, we will all miss you both very much, God speed on your journey home my friends."

The crowd all clapped and the sound of chanting could be heard, "hero's, hero's." Hugging Honk and Gonk with tears in her eyes Grace waved a final goodbye. She took control of the engine and releasing the brakes Chuff began to slowly move away from Imagination World. The sound of cheering soon faded in the distance as the train continued to trundle homeward bound.

6 - Happenings on the Journey Home

On approaching the entrance to the tunnel, the darkness made it seem eerie and the track appeared to go on forever.

"Will we never get home," Grace said to Chuff, "I'm sure the journey didn't seem this far before."

"Yes," said Chuff, "the track was straight on the way in but I thought we had driven through some points a short distance back that has sent us in a curve to the right!"

Chuff was now feeling a bit anxious and said to Grace,

"Maybe not, let's keep going I'm sure it will be ok and we'll see something familiar soon." as he tried to re-assure her.

Unbeknown to Chuff, the hobgoblins had decided to take revenge. Gobby, the leader of the hobgoblins had crept out during the night and switched the points onto a secret track. This would divert Little Chuff and Grace to their side

of the mountain and straight into:
HOBGOBLINS END STATION.

Almost immediately they saw the flare of burning oil lamps which lit up the tunnel, and the flickering dancing shadows made it look even more menacing.

Grace braked furiously and they came to a screeching halt. They were instantly surrounded by vicious hobgoblins clambering on board. Grace let out an ear splitting scream!

She tried to imagine King Snotty and his hobgoblin subjects as kind creatures who might set them free, but found this to be impossible. She made several attempts and it made her head ache. Grace knew this was something her mind could not change no matter how hard or often she tried.

A hoard of hobgoblins each of them baring their teeth and brandishing their sharp black forks and clubs looked treacherous. They were a horrid sight and the smell was so disgusting from their slimy bodies it made Grace retch! Their pointed yellow teeth were decayed and rotten because of their greedy ways gorging themselves daily on fairy cakes. Gobby, came forward and grabbed Grace roughly by the arm and took over the controls of the engine.   Poor Chuff felt helpless.

Gobby, had a small bald head with bulging black eyes and ears that stuck up in the air like an alley cat. The few teeth he had were gold, and he wore a black loin cloth to cover his fat bottom which stuck out a lot, and Grace said,

"Oh, Chuff; I knew things were going too well. What's going to happen to us?"

And he replied, "Have you tried using your imagination?"

"Yes, of course," she bleated, "it's no use...no use at all, we are in deep trouble."

"I think we should keep quiet and hope they don't destroy us....let's pray we will be rescued," Chuff said.

The captured train began to move and very soon they pulled into Hobgoblins End Station.

7 - Hobgoblins End Station

"Get out," the leader commanded to Grace. She was taken by force as she stumbled from the footplate and marched to King Snotty's Castle. Poor Grace found herself in a dark dungeon and thrown into a smelly room. The room had a large window and now terrified she looked out through the bars.

Evil faces peered in at her as she ran across the room to try and hide. They spat and snarled throwing several rats through the bars. Grace froze in terror. Gobby slammed the door shut and she heard the clanging of the huge key locking her in. He shouted,

"We will teach you and that silly engine of yours a lesson you will never forget."

Grace began to cry and Chuff could hear her and he felt completely powerless. In desperation, she tried once again to imagine that the wicked King and his hobgoblin subjects were kind creatures who would let them go. But it was hopeless!

The hobgoblin's who were peering at Grace through the bars thought how ugly human children were and continued to sneer and jeer. The others were covering Chuff with slimy red goo which now dripped down his sad face. They daubed his engine in purple paint shouting,

"Ha, ha, we have you now," pointing their long bony fingers laughing out loud. Just then Grace heard scurrying and sirens going off and let out a scream in terror.

Looking out of the window, she saw King Snotty arriving in a black carriage pulled by a pair of snarling vicious wolves with eyes that glowed like fire. They were fire breathing cunning wolves and as Grace looked at the scene she felt scared stiff! In the past the hobgoblins had seen the wolves in action and they were very afraid. They had seen hobgoblins badly burnt.

Black ravens were hovering overhead looking for trouble and waiting for their chance to swoop down. Vultures perching high close by were watching and waiting hoping to eat the remains of victims. A huge crowd had gathered baring their rotten teeth and brandishing their clubs chanting,

"Destroy them, destroy them," and Grace began to shiver.

The hobgoblins were excited and waiting with bated breath to hear how and when their King would divulge the destiny of the captured pair. Then King Snotty roared,

"Be quiet!" Silence descended as they listened to what he had to say, "My plan is this; we will trade with Queen Saffron, but she has to return Tully and in exchange we will release Little Chuff and Grace."

The crowd all booed, they were not happy as they wanted to see Chuff destroyed and Grace left to rot in the dungeon.

"Shut up!" he shouted angrily, and Willy, one of the wolves on hearing his master speaking in an aggressive tone of voice decided to howl like a banshee into the night air. This set Wally off and he too joined in.

Now, some of the terrified crowd who fearing the King and his wolves fled home. Those remaining began to grumble as they had no choice but to go along with the Kings wishes. He began to speak again,

"We have to choose the sneakiest hobgoblin to take a note to Queen Saffron with our decision," he bellowed.

A voice was heard from the back of the crowd,

"Yes, what have you to say on the matter?" the King said, looking with disdain at a scrawny looking hobgoblin who had spoken.

"My name is Eeeriwig Rat and I will volunteer to do the job as long as you pay me in teeth...your Majesty,"

"TEETH....TEETH," the King snarled.

Now the King was cleverer than Eeeriwig Rat and agreed to pay him with teeth, but not with children's teeth which were valuable. He planned to pay him with teeth which had fallen out of a hobgoblins mouth some time ago. Eeeriwig Rat was a nasty and stupid hobgoblin who thought he could outsmart the King. The hobgoblins knew the King would have the last laugh. The King then said,

"You can have your teeth when the job is done."

The King knew these teeth had no value and sniggered when silly Eeeriwig Rat accepted the deal.

Grace and Chuff were terrified. In their hearts they knew that King Snotty would not honour the agreement even if Queen Saffron were to agree to the deal. They felt hopeless and completely helpless.

Later that night Eeeriwig Rat dragged Grace out of the dungeon and ordered her to start the engine. He stoked up the fire box and they made their way to Imagination World Station. The note delivered read as follows:

We have captured Little Chuff and Grace. By midnight tomorrow if Tully is not returned to us, we will leave Grace to rot in the dungeon and destroy Chuff

Signed

King Snotty of Hobgoblin Land

Arriving in the dead of night to Imagination World Station, the only sound to be heard was the "hoot hoot" from the owls living in a nearby tree. Under the moonlight their big goo goo eyes stared out in curiosity as they wondered what on earth Grace and Chuff were doing back in Fairy Land. The people were fast asleep, and as Eeeriwig Rat jumped off the footplate he left the note pinned prominently on the station door. He then ordered Grace to drive back, and she said,

"I want to go home, please Chuff...do something!"

8 - Queen Saffron Retaliates

The next morning when the Queen received the note from the King she was appalled at what had happened. She immediately called her people to the town square. Reading the words out to the crowd they all roared in anger. The female trolls began crying and Honk's wife, Ponk, said to the Queen in a timid voice,

"Please your Highness, I have a good idea." She wore a pink checked skirt, blouse and hat to match. On her feet were pink checked sandals from which her little fat toes peeped out, and her nails were painted black. Ponk, a clever little creature had been saying to Honk that she knew there could be trouble ahead. The hobgoblins didn't like to be called losers.

"Your Highness," she began, "I was thinking that as the hobgoblins are addicted to our fairy cakes, you could threaten to cut off their supply and they will freak out," she said.

"What a brilliant idea," the Queen replied, "we could offer to supply them with plenty of cakes if they return Grace and Chuff and we keep Tully."

Gark, the leader of the gnomes piped up,

"Yes, why didn't we think of this before and maybe we could have saved Grace and Chuff from their terrible ordeal,"

And she replied,

"You must not forget that the trolls were on their side at that time and they could have used more force against us, but now they no longer can do this."

Gark, and his merry band of men nodded in full agreement.

"Also your Highness," Honk said, "during the past we worked on their side of the mountain trading as carpenters, farmers and toolmakers, why don't we deprive the hobgoblins of all our future services and the logs we provided them with."

"Even better," she replied.

And so it was agreed that a note be sent to King Snotty informing him of this. Now they felt they had the upper hand.

When King Snotty received the message, he gathered his people together to hear what the

Queen had to say. The superior King rejected the proposal immediately and when the crowd heard his decision they went wild.

There were riots in the streets and the evil hobgoblins with their decaying teeth were chanting, "we want our cakes.... we want our cakes,"

There were further protests when they heard about the withdrawal of the other services and the hobgoblins thought the King was mad. Soon the crowd went out of control and Snotty ordered his wolves into action,

"Breathe fire on this stupid lot, I must gain control," he roared.

Mayhem broke out on the streets and the sound of loud drumming could be heard. A number of hobgoblins ran screaming in terror. Those remaining were on fire and the smell of smouldering beards gave off a disgusting stench

of burning hair which filled the air. The wicked ravens saw their chance to join in and came swooping down from the sky pecking out eye balls.

By now the King could see the riot was getting worse, and one of the ravens landed on his head pecking him viciously. He screamed in anger which then forced him to command the fighting be stopped immediately. The wolves skulked away and the ravens flew off munching their eye balls with a glint in their evil mad eyes.

Now the King realised that he would have to give in to Queen Saffron's demands and release the hostages. He ordered a very sullen Gobby to release Grace and Little Chuff immediately. A note was sent straight away to the Queen agreeing to the terms she had demanded.

When the Queen received this news she gathered her people together to inform them of the outcome. The sound of voices triumphantly rang out across the village, "yes, yes, we have won, hurrah, hurrah."

"Yes," she replied, "we have won our battle and our heros will soon be back."

Back in Hobgoblin Land on the King's orders, Gobby hurriedly went to the dungeon to get Grace. A bad tempered and sullen Gobby dragged her out by the hair as she cried and shook in terror, her mind now in turmoil. To her surprise she was bundled onto a very puzzled looking Chuff who was fired up and ready to go! Then he said,

"Good riddance, go now before the King changes his mind," and they headed off at great speed through the tunnel to freedom and back to Fairy Land.

There was much jubilation when the sound of Chuff could be heard emerging from the tunnel. The steam and smoke pouring into the skies was a welcome sight as they arrived. Queen Saffron immediately saw how poor Chuff looked and the dreadful condition he was in. She promptly used her magical powers to return him to his original splendour.

Grace and Chuff were grateful and relieved to have been rescued and back in Fairy Land. They were delighted when they heard that the elders had organised a huge party to celebrate their safe return.

9 - After the Truce

After the festivities, the elders called a meeting to which the Queen attended. The trolls who shared the houses with the fairies and pixies realised it was not a happy situation. The trolls were not the cleanest in their habits and refused to wash, and as you can imagine this had been causing trouble. The fairies and pixies said they had to hold their noses whenever they were near the trolls. The Queen knew that living together in the golden houses had become unsuitable for them all. The trolls needed to build their own homes with logs.

However, some time ago they had run out of logs and other essential supplies when Tully had been stolen. Gark, head of supplies now addressed the Queen and said,

"Your Highness, we are badly in need of wood for the stoves so we can bake our bread, cakes and biscuits. I'm sure you'll all agree that the wonderful smells of baking filling the air every day would be sadly missed if the pixies couldn't cook in the usual traditional manner."

The Queen nodded her head in agreement. She explained to Grace and Chuff that the pixies do not have magical powers. And so it was agreed they would get ready for a trip to Elfin World as soon as possible where they could replenish their supplies.

Little Chuff and Grace listened to these plans and realised their work was not yet over and Grace said,

"We are only too happy to help out on this journey your Highness.... the sooner the better I think."

10 - Preparation & Arrival into Elfin World

Early next morning great activity was taking place. There was no shortage of volunteers, and the work began preparing for the journey ahead. A great friendship had built up between Elfin World and Fairy Land. They were all looking forward to seeing the elves again whom they knew would welcome them with open arms. Stories would be told and much partying would happen throughout the night in Elfin World.

Finally, Chuff and Tully were coupled to several open wagons. Tully was in the front pulling and Chuff in the rear pushing. The passenger's carriage was full of happy volunteers and Queen Saffron was sitting in her magnificent gold carriage with Grace beside her. Her carriage had very large squishy couches to lounge upon, and as Grace sat back savouring delicious goodies provided by the Queen, she decided to find out more about fairy life.

"Your Highness," she began,

"Yes, my child," the Queen replied,

"I was wondering why you are travelling this way and not flying with your beautiful wings which would be easier for you,"

"Well" she said "Our wings are very delicate and fine and using them on long journeys would not be good. Our powers are limited and if we over use them they would dry up.

"That's one of the reasons why we need our precious Tully for these journeys and why I use my gold coach to travel around Fairy Land.

"My people say it makes me look more regal," she continued, and Grace nodded.

As they travelled on their way Grace gazed out of the window enthralled at the views of bridges which spanned silver rivers and trickling streams. She looked in awe at the beautiful countryside as they passed through long dark tunnels that went through mountains. Continuing onwards they came to the edge of a great forest. And slowing down they travelled through a gap which had been cut through the tall trees. In a clearing they saw an impressive station with a shiny silver sign which read:

Elfin Wood Station

On the platform were the most adorable looking creatures that Grace had ever laid eyes on. The elves were tiny and the female's hair tumbled down to their waists. Their faces were delicate and pretty and they had small pointed ears from which dangled long silver earrings. Their uniforms were green and white with large silver buttons marching down the front of their jackets. They wore pointed shoes decorated with big shiny silver buckles that shone in the bright sunshine which was bursting through the clouds. And Grace thought they looked a sight to behold as they stood impatiently waiting for them to disembark.

When Queen Saffron and Grace stepped down, a regal looking elf approached them with welcoming outstretched arms and said,

"Welcome one and all, I am King Effrem and this is Queen Elvira."

They were taller than the other elves and both wore delicate crowns of silver on their heads. The King wore a golden cloak which Grace thought was strange. She wondered why this was as all the rest of his clothing was silver.

The King then turned round and took the young girl's hand who was standing behind him and said,

"This is our daughter, Princess Paris who one day will be crowned Queen of the Elfin World."

Grace looked at her observing she was more beautiful than the others. Her long flowing locks of golden hair cascaded down her back and on her head she wore a silver tiara. Princess Paris began to speak and Grace, now spellbound listened to her every word.

"I am so pleased to meet you, I do hope you had a nice journey, but come now, you all must be hungry and thirsty."

"Please follow us," she said.

Feeling very excited Grace proceeded to follow Queen Saffron and the rest of the party lead by the royals.

Very soon they approached a steep stairway which led to the top of the forest. Grace could see they had built an amazing structure of tree houses. They were built high up in very old oak trees which were linked together with wooden walkways. Grace was eager to see inside and on entering the first tree house she noticed everything was spotlessly clean. Bright colours were painted on the walls and the elves proudly explained that they had made the furniture.

Then Queen Saffron and Grace were ushered to the royal enclosure and into the guest quarters. After they bathed and rested the Queen said,

"You know I rule my kingdom alone and I feel envious of the elfin royals as they share the responsibility of rule. I dream that one day a prince will come along and share my burden."

When Grace heard this story she felt sad for her. She made her mind up that one day soon she would imagine the Queen would meet a caring prince who would make her happy.

A thought then occurred to Grace, and she
asked the Queen why King Effrem's cloak was
the colour of gold when everything else he wore
was silver?

"Well," she began, "when I came here some time ago, I observed the King seemed obsessed with silver. This is not a good thing Grace, so I decided to use my magical powers and change his cloak to gold.

"However, once the change happened the King was absolutely delighted with his golden cloak."

Grace smiled when she heard this explanation and knew the Queen was right,

"How clever of you to think of that your Highness and then to do something about it." And the Queen just smiled.

Just then, a loud gong was heard summoning them to the large banquet which had been laid on in their honour and the sound of pan pipes echoed all over the forest. The pixies had been busy baking their wonderful bread, cakes and biscuits. They had baked them fresh that morning before heading out from Fairy Land. The pixies knew that the elves could not cook in their wooden houses because the risk of fire was too great. And so an abundance of goodies including jellies and exotic fruits were on display at the feast.

Then the King began to speak and they all went quiet,

"My friends, especially our visitors from Fairy Land, please eat, drink and be merry."

Everyone clapped and the King said,

"You will be glad to hear we are pleased to offer Queen Saffron all the logs and wood they require now and in the future."

On hearing this, a cheer went up and they began to party well into the night.

When the moon came up and the stars began to shine, the dancers, musicians and clowns entertained the visitors with their antics. Queen Saffron told the heroic story about the good deeds that Grace and Chuff had done, and how they had rescued Tully. The elves listened enthralled well into the night. Then Grace decided to ask King Effrem why they lived so high up instead of on the forest floor. And he said,

"Well Grace, it's so much brighter living high up in the trees where we are in direct sunlight, whereas down on the forest floor its dark and damp,"

"But why inside the forest at all?" she questioned,

"In your minds all human children think of us as forest and wood dwellers and we are bound by that, but don't feel guilty because we love it here," he said.

By now it was getting very late and the blue moon shining down gave off an air of magical mystery. The eerie shadows it cast down played tricks on their eyes, and the Queen said,

"Time to go Grace, I'm tired, and you must be too."

After a wonderful party and a fabulous time had by all, they trooped back to their tree houses and finally fell asleep in their very soft elfin beds.

11 - Jubilant Journey back to Fairy Land

Bright and early next morning the hard work began. Very soon all the wagons were stacked high with logs and timber and it was time to go back to Fairy Land.

The King, Queen and Princess arrived to wave them off and when they were all fired up and ready to leave, the elves cheered them on their way.

Little Chuff, Grace and Tully were glad to be on the move again. The return journey, although exhausting with the heavy load was very worthwhile. Soon they were back in Fairy Land and they were met by the delighted townsfolk who quickly helped to unload the wood. Happy and very impatient to start building their new homes the trolls were very grateful for all the help they had received. The pixies were busy and scuttled off with trolley loads of wood for their ovens.

That night Queen Saffron invited Grace to sleep in her palace. She lay in a gold four poster bed and as she snuggled down Grace dreamt of home. When she awoke the next morning, she realised she missed her Daddy and felt home sick. After all she thought to herself there is nothing more left for us to do. She knew her friends were at long last happy.

Next morning after a sumptuous breakfast the Queen put her arms around Grace and said,

"You must not blame yourself for all the horrors of hobgoblin world, it's the adults who plant these thoughts in your head with the scary stories they tell you." Grace just smiled and nodded, happily thinking to herself, we will be going home tomorrow.

12 - Going Home

Little Chuff was feeling very excited as he stood on the platform for what he hoped would be his final journey home. The trolls, pixies, fairies and gnomes had re-decorated him with coloured flags. He was missing Igor and had so many stories to tell him about his exciting adventures with Grace. On the hills in the distance a large group of gnomes sitting on their toad stools were now looking sad. They had grown to love Little Chuff and Grace and hoped one day they would meet again.

To the sounds of, "safe journey home, we love you both," ringing in their ears they headed down the track away from Imagination World Station in Fairy Land for the last time.

When they entered the tunnel for home they were both relieved to see the track ran straight ahead. Suddenly, there was a loud bang and Grace shouted,

"Oh no, what now," but then she realised to her delight they had returned to their original size!

Emerging into the bright sunlight which temporarily blinded Grace, she turned away to rub her eyes. On opening them she found to her amazement she was back in the safe comfort of her own bed! The sunshine was streaming through her bedroom window and it was the sun light which had woken her up!

Had this all been a dream she wondered. She quickly got out of bed muttering,

"I must go and see Chuff." She ran to the shed and found Chuff sleeping with a smile on his face, but she noticed there was something else....

He was still bedecked in coloured flags!!!!

The next night snuggling down in her bed, she suddenly remembered her promise to Queen Saffron. She imagined a handsome Prince would arrive in Fairy Land with all the qualities Queen Saffron had wished for.

Thinking of this before drifting off to sleep, she felt a surge of excitement in her tummy and wondered what future adventures she and Chuff would have. Nestling down in the safety of her bed, Grace finally closed her eyes and fell fast asleep.

One morning soon after when Grace woke from her sleep, she found something lying on her pillow....A simple message written on a gold leaf which read:

Thank you my friend, my dreams have come true.

And Grace just smiled.

---The End---

Postscript

Meanwhile back in hobgoblin world with the threat of withdrawal of their beloved fairy cakes the hobgoblins were unable to carry out any evil deeds.

So they came out in the human world. They slithered through cat flaps and climbed through open windows. They pulled cats tails to make them yowl in terror. They poked dogs with long sticks making them bark which would wake whole households.

Jumping up and down on children's beds and pinching babies faces in their cots making them cry out loud giving parents sleepless nights. The children would scream and the hobgoblins would sneak out!

Other favourite larks would be to rattle pots and pans in the kitchen during the night. The poor dads would creep downstairs nervously fearing they were being burgled, only to find the culprits had skulked away.